# Small Brown Dog's Bad Remembering Day

To my family and Stacey – MG

To my mother and my father – BN

First published in hardback in 1999 and paperback in 2000
by Macmillan Children's Books
a division of Macmillan Publishers Limited
25 Eccleston Place, London SW1W 9NF
Basingstoke and Oxford
Associated companies throughout the world
www.panmacmillan.com

ISBN  0 333 74538 8 (HB)
ISBN  0 333 74539 6 (PB)

Text copyright © 1999 Mike Gibbie
Illustrations copyright © 1999 Barbara Nascimbeni

3 5 7 9 8 6 4 2

A CIP catalogue record for this book is available
from the British Library

Printed in Belgium

# Small Brown Dog's Bad Remembering Day

Illustrated by
Barbara Nascimbeni

Story by
Mike Gibbie

MACMILLAN CHILDREN'S BOOKS

Small brown dog was having a really bad remembering day.

He couldn't remember what side to get out of bed.
He couldn't remember what he liked for breakfast.

Worst of all, he couldn't remember his name!
"If only I could find my collar, that would tell
me my name," he said.
But he couldn't remember where he had left it.

He looked high and low for it.
But he couldn't find it anywhere in his kennel.

So he ran outside . . .

. . . and very nearly ran into
Tess the Terrier delivering the post.
"Help, Tess! I've lost my collar
and I don't know WHO I AM!"

"You," said Tess,
"are a small brown dog with a pink nose,
but I don't remember your name."

"Can't you remember anything else?"
asked the small brown dog.
Tess thought hard. "You like splashing in puddles."

"You're right!" said
the small brown dog,
and he set off to find some.

He was
splashing
down the street
when he saw
Dan the Dalmation.
"Help, Dan! I've lost my collar
and I don't know WHO I AM!"

"You," said Dan, "are a small brown dog
with a pink nose,
who likes splashing in puddles,
but I don't remember your name."

"Can't you remember anything else?"
asked the small brown dog.
Dan thought hard. "You're always chasing squirrels."
"You're right!" said the small brown dog,
and he set off for the park.

At the park he ran into
Bobby the Bulldog.
"Help, Bobby! I've lost my collar
and I don't know WHO I AM!"

"You," said Bobby, "are a small brown dog
with a pink nose,
who likes splashing in puddles
and is always chasing squirrels
but I don't remember
your name."

"Can't you remember anything else?"
asked the small brown dog.
Bobby thought hard. "You've got a bad case of fleas."
"You're right!" said the small brown dog,
and he hurried off, scratching.

He went over the road and into the hairdresser's
where he saw Peaches the Poodle.
"Help, Peaches! I've lost my collar
and I don't know WHO I AM!"

"You," said Peaches,
"are a small brown dog
   with a pink nose,
   who likes splashing in puddles,
   is always chasing squirrels and
   has a bad case of fleas,
   but I don't remember your name."

"Can't you remember
anything else?" asked the small brown dog.
Peaches thought hard. "You can't resist hot dogs."
"You're right!" said the small brown dog,
and he remembered that he was hungry.

He turned the corner into the square
where he saw Sid the Sausage dog.
"Help Sid! I've lost my collar and I don't know who I am!"
"You," said Sid, "are a small brown dog with a pink nose,
who likes splashing in puddles, is always chasing squirrels,
has a bad case of fleas and can't resist hot dogs,
but I don't remember your name."

"Can't you remember anything else?"
asked the small brown dog.
Sid thought hard. "You bury bones in the sand."
"You're right!" said the small brown dog,
and he set off to dig one up.

He went across the square
and into the building site where
he saw Ralph the Rottweiler.
"Help, Ralph! I've lost my collar
and I don't know WHO I AM!"

"You," said Ralph,
"are a small brown dog
with a pink nose,
who likes splashing in puddles,
is always chasing squirrels,
has a bad case of fleas,
can't resist hot dogs and
buries bones in the sand,
but I don't remember your name."

"Can't you remember anything else?"
asked the small brown dog.
Ralph thought hard. "You blow a big shiny trumpet."
"You're right!" said the small brown dog,
and he set off to join his band.

He went over the hill and into the park
where he saw Charlie the Chihuahua.
"Help, Charlie! I've lost my collar
and I don't know WHO I AM!"

"You," said Charlie,
"are a small brown dog
with a pink nose,
who likes splashing in puddles,
is always chasing squirrels,
has a bad case of fleas,
can't resist hot dogs,
buries bones in the sand and
blows a big shiny trumpet,
        but I don't remember your name."

"Can't you remember
anything else?"
asked the small brown dog.
Charlie thought hard.
"You're always losing your collar."
"I know that!" said the small brown dog,
"But where can I find it?"
"You could try the police station," said Charlie.
"You're right!" said the small brown dog,
and he set off to do just that.

He ran back through the park, over the road,
up the street and into the police station,
where Alf the Alsatian was standing behind the desk.
"Help, Alf! I've lost my collar and . . ."

"Here it is!" said Alf. "Roger the Retriever
brought it in this morning."
"At last I remember," said the small brown dog.

"I'm a small brown dog
with a pink nose,

who likes splashing in puddles,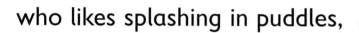

is always chasing squirrels,

has a bad case of fleas,

can't resist hot dogs,

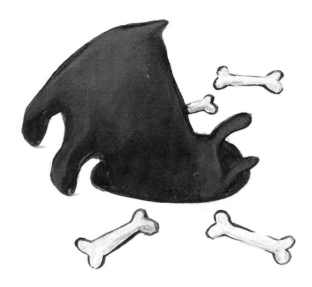

buries bones in the sand,

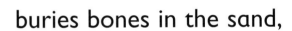

blows a big shiny trumpet

and is always losing his collar,
and my name is . . ."

"But I could have told you that!"